The Mother Goose Show

Classic Rhymes
Re-told by David Messick and the Rainbow Puppets
Illustrated by Liu Light

Dedicated to
Jane Elmore
and all the other terrific early childhood teachers we've encountered.

The Mother Goose Show
© 2022 / All Rights Reserved
By David Messick
Featuring traditional rhymes and characters
Original Illustrations by Lucia Liu
Puppet Images Rainbow Productions, Inc.

Puppets created by Laura Baldwin, Chris Frank, and Jill Harrington

Rainbow puppeteers include James Cooper, Wesley Huff, Alyssa Jones, and David & Joshua Messick

ISBN: 978-1-7332484-7-1
Third printing / Printed in the USA
Rainbow Puppet Publications 18 Easthill Court, Hampton, Virginia 23664
Rainbow Puppet Productions is a non-profit, educational entertainment company

Thanks to:
Curtis Johnson, Traci Massie, Erin Matteson, and Optima Health
Laura Baldwin, Tony Gabriele, Jim & Linda Haas and the Academy of Dance and Gymnastics,
David & Stephanie Messick, Marcy Messick, Nancy Kent Swilley, and Rose West.

Mother Goose jumped out of her chair
The moment that she heard
There were folks who just did not know
Her famous rhyming words.

She sounded the alarm
And told her friends throughout the land,

"We really must respond.
So, help me come up with a plan."

B.B. Wulf replied,
"Let's visit towns from far and near."

Humpty Dumpty said,
"We'll tell our rhymes for all to hear."

Then Mother Goose said, "That sounds great...
That's how the folks will know.
We'll tell our rhymes
and stories in a great big trav-ling show!"

They loaded sets and costumes...
   Everything their trunks could hold.
And when the curtains opened
   Here's the stories that they told:

Humpty Dumpty sat on a wall

Humpty Dumpty had a great fall

All the king's horses
    And all the king's men
        Couldn't put Humpty together again.

There once was woman
Who lived in a shoe
She had so many children
She didn't know what to do.

Jack and Jill went up the hill
To fetch a pail of water.

Jack fell down and broke his crown
And Jill came tumbling after.

Hickory, dickory, dock,
    The mouse ran up the clock.

The clock struck one,
The mouse ran down
Hickory, dickory, dock.

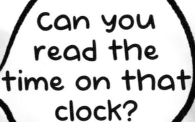

Can you read the time on that clock?

I just look at my phone!

Little Bo Peep has lost her sheep
   And doesn't know where to find them.

Leave them alone and they'll come home.
Bringing their tails behind them.

Little Miss Muffet sat on her tuffet
Eating her curds and whey.

Along came a spider
 And sat down beside her
  And frightened Miss Muffet away.

A tuffet is a little stool.

Curds and whey are cottage cheese!

I'm not really scared of spiders. I even sing songs about them!

The itsie-bitsie spider
    Went up the water spout.

Down came the rain
    And washed the spider out.

Out came the sun
And dried up all the rain

And the itsie-bitsie spider
Went up the spout again!

Old King Cole was a merry old soul
   And a merry old soul was he.

He called for his pipe
   And he called for his bowl
      And he called for his fiddlers of three.

23

Rub-a-dub dub
Three men in a tub
A butcher, a baker, a candlestick maker.

Rub-a-dub dub
Three men in a tub
They're all so squeaky clean!

Hey, diddle, diddle,
The cat and the fiddle.
The cow jumped over the moon.

The little dog laughed
  To see such a sight
    And the dish ran away with the spoon.

Twinkle, twinkle little star
How I wonder what you are.
Up above the world so high,
Like a diamond in the sky.

Twinkle, twinkle little star
How I wonder what you are.

I usually howl at the moon, but tonight I feel like singing!

They sang and danced with
B.B. Wulf until the very end.

And now so many more know
Mother Goose and all her friends.

31

For many years, the Rainbow Puppets have presented Mother Goose and her famous rhymes. Perhaps we will see you at a performance of "The Mother Goose Show."